THE BUNNY HOP

By Sarah Albee
Illustrated by Maggie Swanson

Featuring Jim Henson's Sesame Street Muppets

A GOLDEN BOOK • NEW YORK

Published by Golden Books Publishing Company, Inc., in conjunction with
Children's Television Workshop

A portion of the money you pay for this book goes to
Children's Television Workshop. It is put right back into
SESAME STREET and other CTW educational projects.
Thanks for helping!

A funny thing happened on Sesame Street
One Easter, not long ago.
Bees were buzzing and birds were singing.
The flowers were starting to grow.

Elmo woke up and yawned and said,
"It's a beautiful, sunny day!"
Then he went to put on his slippers
And one of them hopped away!

As Ernie was reading the paper,
Something furry hopped over the funnies.
When Bert went to start the spring cleaning,
The closet was chock-full of bunnies!

Grover was playing baseball.
A rabbit was under his cap.

Herry was coloring Easter eggs.
A bunny leaped into his lap!

While Zoe was planting her garden,
She found bunnies filling her shed.

As Cookie was looking for jelly beans,
He found bunny rabbits instead.

Where had these bunnies come from?
Nobody really knew.
Oscar found three in his trash can!
What was a grouch to do?

Hoots was playing his saxophone
When out of it popped a bunny.

As Prairie Dawn ate her cereal,
A rabbit knocked over the honey!

"What's going on?" people shouted.
"It's becoming a funny habit.
Every time we turn around
We find a bunny rabbit!"

Big Bird rounded the corner.
Here's what they heard him say—
"Has anyone seen my bunnies?
They seem to have run away!"

He sat on the stoop and said sadly,
"They were all in this basket I made!
They must've jumped out of this hole here.
Who will hop in the Easter parade?"

Then he noticed his friends holding bunnies,
So he handed each one a hat.
"Let's all go and march together!" he said. . . .

And everyone did just that!